Quips and Quaint Sayings in English

By
Rose Wolfe Osmondson

Rose Wolfe Osmondson

First printing, May, 2008

ISBN 978-0-6152-0351-5
Published by AllawayBooks
www.allawaybooks.com

Printed by Lulu in the United States of America
www.lulu.com

Author's Foreword

My maiden name was Rose Glidewell and I went to school in Limon, Colorado until 1926. We moved to Seminole and Dad worked for the Amerada Oil Co.

In 1932 I married P. B. Wolfe and he worked for the Sinclair Oil Co. The moved us a lot. We retired in Pawhuska, Oklahoma in 1965 and moved to Yakima, Washington in 1969 to take care of my aging mother. P. B. passed away in 1976.

I went to Carlsbad in 1989 to become guardian for my aging cousin Mabel Sizemore. In 1996 I married Floyd Osmondson later moving back to Yakima., but Floyd passed away in 2003. I have lived alone since then.

I lost my vision in 2000 and have had to have help.

Timothy Gonderman has helped me the past year. He has written a book called *The Weary Traveler* on his exploits with Satan and his deliverances there from. It is a very good book.

I trust this book will be a blessing to all that read it and bring back memories like it did for me.

Rose Wolfe Osmondson
Yakima, WA
April 4, 2008

Rose

Publisher's Foreword

Rose Osmondson was 97 years young when she approached me with the idea of publishing a book. She is one amazing Christian lady.

I first met Rose in adult Sunday school class at the Stone Church Assembly of God in Yakima. No matter what the lesson, Rose always had a positive word or a relative Scripture verse to add. Sometimes I thought the instructor planned it that way. When Rose could not attend our class, things sometimes went a little flat.

I think she has memorized the tune and lyrics to just about every Christian hymn that I have ever heard.

This book she has written contains anecdotes, and quotable quotes, some that have been around for years; many that the current generations have never heard and some that we older generations have forgotten.

Viva la Rose!

Al Allaway, Publisher

Quips and Quaint Sayings in the English Language

(Organized in no specific order)

Life without a friend is death without a witness.

Anger is like a viper, you never know how, when, or where it is going to strike and it can be deadly.

Sometimes you do not know where your bread is buttered.

Just plodding along, singing along..

Crooked as a barrel of snakes

Finances are out of whack.

Where's the beef?

Many happy returns of the day

Hanging loose

Hang in there!

Holy Moley!

When at night you cannot sleep, talk to the Shepherd and stop counting sheep.

Glory be!

Stay put

Shut your mouth

Shut up

Heavenly days, Heavenly daze.

Button your lip

Peace is not the absence of conflict, but the presence of God no matter what the conflict.

Toot your horn

I opened my mouth and put my foot in it.

Some things are better left unsaid.

Things are going my way.

Hunky dorey!

Ho, Ho, Hum...

Warm and fuzzy

Dry as gun powder

Fresh as the morning dew

Rotten to the core

A kind word is like a Spring day.

It was only a sunny smile,
And little it cost in the giving.
But like morning light, it scattered the night,
And made the day worth living.

Scared me to death

Sharp as a pencil

Bald as a billiard ball

Hollow as a pumpkin

Tricks to the trade

Skid row.

Slick as a hog on ice

Black sheep of the family

Don't forget which side the bread is
buttered on!

A shirt tailed relative.

Gentle as a breeze

He got his come uppens!

Johnny come lately

Fuss budget

Button up your upper lip

Just plain vanilla

Bold as a lion

Sometimes we win for losing

Howdy doody

Talk is cheap

Put your money where your mouth is.

Goose feathers

A stitch in time saves nine!

Short fuse

The long haul

Smart alec

Wise as an owl

Driving me crazy

A night mare

High as a kite

Go fly a kite!

Sit on a tack.

Cool as a cucumber

Sharp as a razor

Easy as pie

Grumpy as an old man

Piece of cheese cake

Have your cake and eat it too.

Sour as kraut

Light as a feather

Heavy as lead

Break my heart

Miraculous deliverances

Life is a mystery

A lot is involved

Curiosity killed the cat

Not my piece of cake (or my cup of tea)

Stupid as an ox

Without friends no one would choose to live, though he had everything else.

Back to the drawing board

Back to square one

Not going to bank on it!

Flies off the handle

Mark those that cause division among you, and avoid them.

Birds of a feather flock together.

Get your mind out of the gutter.

Pretty as a picture

On a gravy train

At the grass roots

Down to the bare facts

Super duper!

What is the catch?

When the enemy comes in like a flood, the spirit of the Lord lifts up a standard against him.

How come you did that?

Come Holy Spirit, we need you!

The shadow box

The large painting

Let's call it a day!

Bread and butter

Set the woods on fire

I do not feel up to par.

Par for the course

Man's best support is a very dear friend

Slick as snot on a door knob

Make a little spark

So close that you cannot see the forest for
the trees.

Goes like a big rig

Borrow trouble

Put the cart before the horse.

Kissing cousins

Bread winner

A laughing hyena

Laughter is like a dose of medicine.

The pen is mightier than the sword.

Pulled a boo boo

The old goat

He is a crab

The old buzzard

Not for the faint hearted

*God has many names, though He is only
one Being.*

Hard-headed Hannah!

Pete and repeat

Jump the gun

Pitch a little woo

Make Whoopee

Everything is coming up roses

Wait and see

Hurry up, and wait!

Better late than never

When we lose God, it is not God who is lost.

I wonder what is next?

Next to nothing

Good gracious!

My word!

Had to learn the hard way

Tiddely winks

Every day is just like Christmas!

Piddling job

Tinkering around

Sponging off someone

Don't push me around!

He is too old to cut the mustard anymore.

Old fuddy duddy

Belly up!

Keep your distance

Tooth and toe nail

Mind boggling

Easy come, easy go!

Run into a snag

Clear the deck

That gives me the willies!

Wise as a serpent, harmless as a dove

Some people talk about finding God, as if
He could get lost.

He that winneth souls is wise.

Hot as the blazing sun

Run it into the ground

The light hearted

Going big guns

Top of the list

Since heck was a pup

That's for me to know and you to find out!

What we are is God's gift to us. What we become is our gift to God.

Been through the ropes

I have bigger fish to fry.

You make a better door than a window!

Goody two-shoes

Let's get the ball rolling!

Get their feathers ruffled

Like buying a pig in a poke!

In a peck of trouble

A peck on the cheek and a hug around the
neck

He is up the creek.

Ears like a jack rabbit

They ripped their own britches!

Pass the buck

Money coming in like hand over fist

It sounds fishy to me!

Catty wumpus

Pleased as punch

Talk your ear off

I am no dumb bunny!

The Devil's advocate

Witches brew

A dumb waiter

Ace in the hole

No big deal

I do not know what the score is

Wishful thinking

It was a tear jerker

My eye lids are heavy

Beauty is only skin deep

Fear knocked at the door. Faith answered.
And lo, no one was there!

Flighty as a grasshopper

Three sheets to the wind

The straw that broke the camel's back

Dirty bird!

Whistling Dixie!

You cannot put a band-aid on a broken
arm, it just does not work!

The hand writing on the wall

Things are really stacking up!

Quit, cold turkey

The proof is in the pudding

Young whipper-snapper

That is hog-wash!

Turn about is fair play

*The will of God will not take you where the
grace of God cannot keep you.*

Jitter-bug

Same old turn around

A piece of cake

Pie in the sky

Old Mother Hubbard

Johnny fair play

Johnny jump-up

Jumping jehoshephat

Bless me bagpipe, curse me kilt

Kill joy!

Out of this world

Time, Why did you punish me?

Hit the jackpot

Jeepers creepers, where'd you get those
peepers (sneakers)?

I had to eat a piece of humble pie

Lolly gagger

An onery old cuss

From the frying pan into the fire

No brag; just facts

Just another manic Monday

That stopped the clock!

Say nope to dope

Make a mountain out of a mole hill

You are always over reacting

Everybody and his brother will be there

Everybody needs a nest egg

Nip it in the bud

Let your conscience be your guide
He's always on the fence

Just do it!

Cost you an arm and a leg

Put a fork in me and turn me over because
I am done.

It may sky rocket

Get it done, Skeeter!

Have some wrinkles to be ironed out

Money in the bank

Prayer changes things

Honey do this, honey do that, HONEY DO

Going to hit the crow's nest

Good for the goose is good for the gander

Had a run away

Had a tough day

Until the cows come home

It backfired!

Split the blanket

If the bed is not rocking, divorce is knocking.

Pie in the sky

God tells us to burden Him with whatever burdens us.

Living high on the hog

Oh! Rasberries!

Keep a stiff upper lip

A poker face

Keep it real do not be phony

Can't cut it with hot butter

I've heard that umpteen times!

Fake it till you make it

The point of no return

Johnny on the spot

Got teed off

Blab it and grab it

A little dab will do you

When the knees are not often bent, the feet soon slide.

I see a red flag!

Hold your horses

He's a panty waist

He is a milk toast

Put me on the spot

The silent majority

Light as a feather

Don't take a wooden nickel

Put up your dukes

Cold turkey

He means well

Easy is as easy does

Misery loves company

That is a bummer!

Not up to snuff

A vessel is broken on the potter's wheel

Winken, Blinken and Nod went out to sea.

If it is not broken, do not fix it

Left out in the rain

Everything is going my way

Not worth his salt

Can't beat that with an ugly stick

Drunk as a skunk

Have a sharp tongue

We had a ball

Over the hill

That's all she wrote!

When my ship comes in

It would sell like hot cakes

You've opened a real can of worms!

Give me an 'e' for effort

Give them an inch; they take a mile

Inch by inch everything is a cinch; yard by yard it is hard.

The wheel of God grinds slowly, but grinds exceedingly fine.

It got swept under the carpet

All in a nut shell!

Merciful days

Every dog has his day

And the bottom fell out!

Hotter than blue blazes

Goody, goody gum drop!

Cannot read your mind

Where the rubber meets the road

I have a jillion ideas!

I would not touch that with a ten foot pole!

It took all that to bring about this

If it does not come out in the wash, it will come out in the rinse.

That is out of the picture

Picture perfect

It did not last long

Cut off his tail to spite his face

Got his tail caught in the lawn mower

Been around the block a few times

I'm not surprised, but sadly disappointed

Been there and done that!

God has a way of revealing things to us

Do not put the cart before the horse

Gone to Hell in a hand basket

A stitch in time saves nine

We reap what we sow

God does not settle His account in October
or August

Where is the fire?

Where there is smoke there is fire

White as a ghost

Money does not grow on trees

That takes a load off of my back

Do not butt your head agaist the wall

I haven't seen that in a coons age

Do not burst my bubble

Driving me batty

Tore up the cob house

Butter me up

Sock it to me, kiddo!

All the hoodlums in the country

Sour as vinegar

Happy as a lark

What's cooking?

Foot loose and fancy free

Don't let the bird out of the cage

Free as a bird

Close the barn door after the horse is gone

Leave all your troubles behind

Going to church is like taking a bath; it leaves you fresh and clean.

Try it, you'll like it

Do not hash your troubles; nobody cares!

Warning: This book is not for the weak in spirit or faint hearted

Fight your own battles

Do not push the button too far

The well never runs dry

That's cutting it pretty fine

Made in the shade

Almost always counts in horseshoes and grenades

Never too old to learn; I am learning more every day.

Are you my sugar daddy?

A change in the wind

Save it for a rainy day

Dark as midnight

Light as the midday sun

Moonlight and roses bring memories of you.

Shot his wad

Where the rubber meets the road

Sweet as sugar or honey

Wait 'till I get a round <u>Tuit</u>

Talking like a jay bird

A round-about way

Grandpa hit the hay (hit the sack)

Put up your dukes!

On easy street

When our ship comes in

Cooking up a storm

Do not stir me up

Fast as a race horse

Slow as a turtle

Down on their luck

Keep me posted

Price is sky rocketing

Strong as horse hair

Fowl mouthed

Johnny on the spot

Join the club

Good gracious!

Tarred and feathered

Run out of town on a rail

In the depths of despair

Cast your bread upon the waters

Jealousy is cruel as the grave

Left holding the sack (bag)

Are you holding out on me?

Using me to their advantage

He hit the nail on the head

Course as sand paper

Smooth as glass

They made a shipwreck of their lives.

Sweet as peaches

He is a cheap skate

It is an uphill pull (climb)

That is a down hill fall

A free taxi, if you ask me

Handy as a pocket in a shirt

He is a screw ball

She is a nit-picker!

Little is much when God is in it

Take it one day at a time

I'm hotter than a firecracker

We have second thoughts

By the skin of my teeth

The height of stupidity

Nip and tuck

Chit or chat

That's a very hard life

Nothing is too hard for God

To dream of the person you would like to be
is to waste the person you are.

If two agree it shall be done

Smooth as a sow's ear

Hard as a baseball bat

It is in the process (The check is in the
mail)

In due time

The well ran dry

Soft as a whisper

Get off the ground floor

Cozy as a bear

Trip the light fantastic

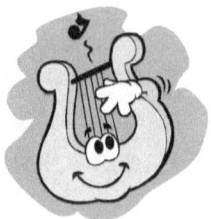

Let the music begin!

Slippery as a banana peel

Shoot the sherbet to her Herbert!

Tiny as a mustard seed

Who cut the cheese?

Open the door, Richard!

Jibbering idiot

Loose as a goose

Happy days are here again

Stubborn as a mule

Ready to throw in the towel

Get your priorities in the right place

Top of the line

Pickled me to death

He beat the socks off me

I'm a slow poke

Jump down my throat...

Back off!

So close, yet so far

Knew her like a book

It's not the end of the world

Would you give me a hand?

A poker face

Sharp as a razor's edge

Dull as a knife

Dumber than a fence post

Too dull to cut butter

Give us a wake up call

Wobbles like a duck

Yankee Doodle went to town, riding on his pony. He put a feather in his hat and called it macaroni.

Crazy as a loon

Explore the territory

Easy come, easy go

Fits like a glove

Where there is a will, there is a way

It's like a boomerang; it comes back to you.

Flat as a pancake (or a board)

Get your mind out of the gutter

Constantly rubbing me the wrong way

Putting salt into your wounds

Can't put a square peg in a round hole

I've been put through the wringer

Wise as a serpent

I'm looking over a four leaf clover, that I
overlooked before...

Dry as powder

Warm as toast

Hard as the rock of Gibralter

Come and go; hustle and bustle

He is a worry wart

She is a wet blanket

Who's the wall flower?

Cooking with gas

Cleaning up the dirt

Airing out your dirty laundry

At my wit's end

It can be a never ending process

Give or take a little bit and something has to give...

Scratch me off your list

Put it on the back burner

It is a done deal!

I'm danged if I do, and danged if I don't

If wishes were fishes, we'd all be rich

That is scumumptuous

You cannot win for losing

I'll be out of here like Lottie's eye

Okay, Hosea

Who spilled the beans?

Keep your cotton-picking hands off...

Keep your distance

Bridle your tongue

Welcome with open arms

Keep your mind occupied

An idle mind is the Devil's workshop

They blew their stack

Love suffers long and is still kind

Drop it like a hot potato

A living dog is better than a dead lion...

Worry is like a rocking chair, a lot of
action, but going nowhere.

It is sugar coated

Get out of my hair

That's not the half of it

Get the monkey off my back.

Add fuel to the fire

Everything is topsy turvy

Look for the pot of gold at the end of the rainbow.

Talk is cheap

Chalk it up   Wipe the slate clean

Cooking with gas

It's mind boggling

Hush puppy

Walking the floor over you

Walking the chalk line

This is just the talking stage

She's a pillar of stone

What's the score?

Turn over a new leaf

Don't rob the cradle

The cow jumped over the moon

Moon over Miami

Look for a needle in a haystack

See you in a while, crocodile!

He's a pinch penny. – a tight wad

He's so tight, he squeaks when he walks.

A hobby horse   A moron

Tight-fisted   A book-worm

A couch-potato

She has a bun in the oven

A bread basket

The rain caused a real gully-washer

A good listener is like a rubber band; it stretches...

What's the point?

Don't cross the bridge until you come to it.

The point is not to bother

Fool's gold

Slick Willy

Like a sore thumb

Hang nail   Bust bosom

It rained on my parade

Plump rump   Pill-box hat

Brown derby hat   Wind breaker jacket

A corn cob pipe

A stool pigeon

A kisket, a casket, my red & yellow basket

I'm having a hard time getting off the
ground floor.

Let well enough alone

Are you pulling my leg?

He twisted my arm and made me do it.

I'm pulling the strings

A penny for your thoughts

Come clean!

Seeing is believing

Somewhere over the rainbow!

*Spirituality is... the awareness that
survival is the savage fight between you
and yourself.*

If it is to be, it is up to me.

Going down hill pretty fast

An ace in the hole

Back to Timbuktu

June in January

Tie the knot

Weight is what broke the wagon down

Too many cooks spoil the broth

He got carted away

We're all under the weather

Mad as a wet hen (..a swatted hornet)

Let's drop it!

At the drop of a hat...

Quick as a flash

If you get a lemon, make lemonade.

The Ugly Duckling   Blind as a bat

So close, yet so far...

No Hanky-panky!

A little bird told me

That's not according to Hoyle!

It's for the birds

I flubbed up!

It was a hair raising event

She's a blabber mouth

Loose lips sink ships

It will be a rocky road

Something fishy about it

Sticky fingers

Red as a rooster's comb

The love of money is the root of all evil.

Is your glass half full, or half empty?

She is wishy-washy

Go for it!   Jump off the deep end!

People do not see eye to eye

As long as there are two, there will be two opinions.

Silence is golden!

Up the creek without a paddle

He is not worth his salt

Good grief!

The spirit is willing but the flesh is weak.

Our strength is made perfect in weakness.

Step on too many toes...

They that wait upon the Lord shall renew their strength, they shall mount up as wings of eagles, they shall walk and not be weary, they shall run and not faint. Teach me, teach me Lord to wait.

It is a thousand wonders that I did not break anything

Rotten to the core

We cannot diagnose every case, but we can find the remedy.

Ready to go, ready to stay, ready my place to fill, ready for service lowly or great, ready to do His will.

It does not take a rocket scientist to figure that out!

Just another statistic

Every little whisper...

I came over a big hurdle

Going big guns

It's off to a flying start

Hold 'er Newt, she's a raring...

Money talks

Bless your little pea-pickin' heart

Heavenly days

Drat it!

Easy little fellow, it will be alright...

Stirring up a storm   Talking up...

Shift gears

Let bygones be bygones

Let's not dwell on it

Saving up for a rainy day

Jiminy Crickets!

Busy as a bee

Lost my thought with a mental block

A bucket full of wishes

Windy Jim

Sticky as fly paper

Like a fish out of water

Mad as an old wet hen

Not yet dry behind the ears

See you later, alligator!

Get 'er done!

Actions speak louder than words

Keep it real

It is a great life if you do not weaken, but
sometimes I weaken.

Go jump in the lake!

Go take a hike!

He pulled his own weight

Are you walking on thin ice?

We can read between the lines

Wit's end corner

Fuss budget

He's pussy footing around

Why prolong the agony?

No matter how thin you slice it, it is still
baloney!

Having fun at everyone else's expense

Don't get so uptight about everything

Sometimes solving one problem creates
two more.

Busy as a bee

Hard as a coconut

Tribulation worketh patience

A hound dog pup

Chomping at the bit

It's not the end of the world

It's not written in stone!

Pass the bit, please

Dream in the process of coming true

We have to smooth out the edges

It's the power of suggestion!

Move it up a tab

Something is rotten in Denmark

A loftier purpose

Shine your bald head for a quarter

I do not give a hoot

He has a charley horse

Will power is important

Kick rocks!

We are getting squared away

Between a rock and a hard place

It can boggle your mind

Raining cats and dogs

Gooney bird

Boar's nest   Grizzly Adams

The kid was plum loco

Beat the street

Ugly as a coon dog

Straight as an arrow

Pushing up daisies

Rough as a cob

Quit beating the dead horse

Sour as a lemon

Sour puss

It was a gravy train

Beyond the point of no return

If it was a snake, it would have bit you!

Bored to tears

So quiet you could hear a pin drop

Let her rip, tater chip!

Don't bust yer buttons!

Words fitly spoken are like apples of gold
in pitchers of silver.

Run the gauntlet

Fuzzy as a peach

Skinned alive!

Totally out of kilter

This is not ordinary weather, what is the
ordinary?

You can loose your mind over many
things; the devil will see to that.

I'm not a mind reader

It's a matter of mind over matter

You know what I mean, jelly bean

Let bygones be bygones

Cold as a potato

Drat it or praise the Lord!

Dad burned it!

Oh, heavenly days!

Nurse or a purse

Good night, nurse

Like a galloping goose

Like a bana belt...

Everything is coming up roses

Let old dogs lay

Silent but deadly

Pull in your puckering string

Cross that bridge when you get to it

Kick, gravel and travel

A nagging woman is like a dripping faucet.

There are two sides to every coin

A bird in the hand is worth two in the bush.

You would argue with a signpost, if I was the signpost.

Crazy as a bed-bug

Nutty as a fruit cake

Let the right hand know what the left hand is doing.

Kicked to the curb

That's pretty far fetched!

Slow as molasses in the dead of winter

He was stacking up brownie points

A thorn in the flesh

Zippity doo dah

That is not my cup of tea

Have you lost your cotton picking mind?

Sitting on the stool of do nothing

Cream puff religion

That is a settled fact

Having second thoughts?

Gentle as a breeze

Let her go, Gallaher!

I do not want to put a cog in the wheel

We have to make it!

All at once

But it is still perking

She is a-going, Jesse

Many happy returns of the day

Strain at a mule heel, swallow a camel

Don't count your chickens before the eggs
are hatched.

Works like a horse

Keep your mind occupied

Mine went south on me

About to catch up to you

Fast as a race horse

Loud as a March hare

Nothing to write home about

Just raking them in

A poet and did not know it

Our minds go in the same direction

Don't be a fibber fox

If you lie, you fly; if you burn, you will turn

Everything is fouled up

She got canned

Bleeding me to death

Your guess is as good as mine

His mind is at the bottom of the barrel.

Right now things are looking rather bleak,
but it is always darkest just before dawn...

Let's turn the card over

He is the laughing stock

It sticks out like a sore thumb

Hubba, hubba; hurry up!

Phoney baloney

We need him like a hole in the head

Here you are at ground zero; there is no
place but up.

Do not put junk in the trunk

I never met your equal before

I can beat you at your own game

Don't cry over spilled milk

God made your worst enemy become your best friend; I have seen it happen.

Do not push the issue

Please don't pick me to pieces

Bygones are like water under the bridge

Skin me alive

Pleased as punch

Stop mouthing off

I am thrilled to pieces

Put the pedal to the metal

For crying out loud!

Nobody will put up with your idiosyncrasies

Flap on the old feed bag

Enough said

Yaddity yaddity

That is par for the course

Well, I'll be a monkey's uncle!

The early bird gets the worm

Curiosity killed the cat

It was dead in the water

He already kicked the bucket

That did not prove much

It is the end of the rainbow

There is a light at the end of the tunnel

Don't rock the boat

Strike a match   When pigs fly

Pucker your cheek

I do not want to steal your thunder

Do not step on my toes

He is so stubborn and rebellious and set in his ways, that a stick of dynamite could not change him; but God can.

Prayer is our greatest weapon but most people do not use it until the last resort.

You cannot teach an old dog new tricks

I am kinda out of snuff today

Put your money where your mouth is

You have to feed a man's ego to get along with him better.

Men should be like a good cup of coffee, strong and hot.

Women should be like a warm kitten, snug and cuddly.

The luck of the Irish

Bless your little pea-picking heart

I do not want to jump the gun

God delays, but doesn't forget.

It's as scarce as hen's teeth

It takes effort to be gracious

Another in the nitch of life

Dig in our heels and press on

So broke I cannot pay attention

I've got my nose to the grind stone

She can't hold a candle to me

He's got a photographic memory

Get off your high horse!

Haste makes waste

That's over kill

He is a kill joy

Who let the cat out of the bag?

Better late than never

School days, school days, good old golden rule days. Reading and writing and 'rithmatic, taught to the tune of a hick'ry stick. You were my queen in calico, I was your bashful barefoot beau. I wrote on my slate, "I love you so," when we were a couple of kids.

They nickel and dime me to death

We've got the tiger by the tail

Sorry, but that is the way the cookie crumbles

Just a thimble full

That sure got his goat

It's puppy love!   They are smooching

Leaping Lena   Love is blind

Running around like a chicken with its
head cut off

She got the jitters

Gave up the ghost, he died

Circumstances put a kink in my affairs

And it gave me goose pimples down my
back

*Faith sees the invisible, believes the
incredible and receives the impossible.*

Drove me bronco

He lost his cookies

In the wild blue yonder

If Pickled Penny picked a peck of pickled
pickles, how many pickled pickles did
Pickled Penny pick?

By hook or by crook

Living high on the hog

He has cut out some of his ornery ways

And that's hog wash

A rough old codger

Don't ream me out!

And don't give me any backtalk

Is it in You?

Let your conscience be your guide, as you
wobble from side to side.

The fury in a pheasant's wings

Go to bed with Arthur (..itis) and get up
with Ben (..gay)

I told a man I had colored blood in me; can
he figure that out? (Answer to the riddle: It's red!)

There's a railroad crossing without any
cars; Can you spell that without any R's?
(Answer to the riddle: T H A T!)

Writing up a storm!

I'm going to catch me a cold!

Like a whirl wind

There are no big I's or little U's here

If you sprinkle when you tinkle, be a
sweetie and clean the seatie.

I'm climbing the walls!

Are you so far in debt that you can't see
daylight?

Like a blind goose in a hail storm

Oh, My foot!

Money talks and B.S. walks!

Bite your tongue

Charge it to the dust and let the rain settle
it!

Stay away from fist city!

It's like robin's egg blue

Sharp as a bowling ball, dummy!

She got a tongue lashing

Set the woods on fire, make a small spark

She lost her marbles

Dry as powder; wet as a sponge

A bushel and a peck and a hug around the neck

Shifting gears

In it to win it!

Turn the record over

Curly que

Holy Moley, glory be: Marinatha, JESUS is coming!

All images licensed from Broderbund *CLICK ART Christian Graphic Deluxe*

Quips and Quaint Sayings

www.ingramcontent.com/pod-product-compliance
Lightning Source LLC
Chambersburg PA
CBHW031901170626
46807CB00004B/1831